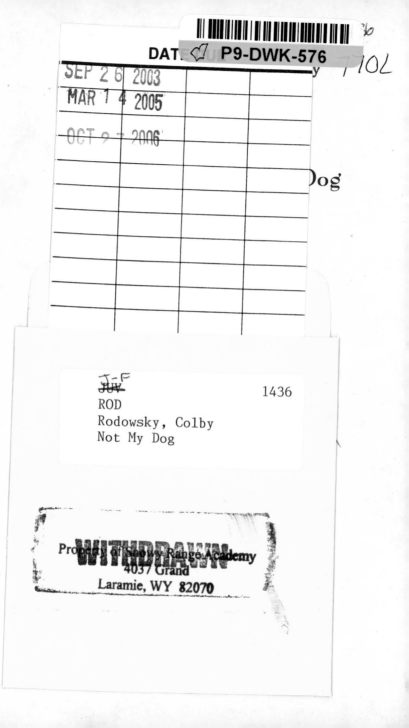

# Not My Dog

## COLBY RODOWSKY

PICTURES BY THOMAS F. YEZERSKI

A SUNBURST BOOK ⋈ FARRAR STRAUS GIROUX

Text copyright © 1999 by Colby Rodowsky
Illustrations copyright © 1999 by Thomas F. Yezerski
Distributed in Canada by Douglas & McIntyre Ltd.
Printed in the United States of America
First edition, 1999
Sunburst edition, 2001
10 9 8 7 6 5 4 3 2

Library of Congress Cataloging-in-Publication Data
Rodowsky, Colby F.
    Not my dog / Colby Rodowsky : pictures by Thomas F. Yezerski. — 1st ed.
      p.   cm.
    Summary: Eight-year-old Ellie has to give up her life-long dream of getting a puppy
after her parents agree to take in the dog that Great-aunt Margaret can no longer keep.
    ISBN 0-374-45538-4 (pbk.)
    [1. Dogs—Fiction. 2. Great-aunts—Fiction.] I. Yezerski, Thomas, ill. II. Title.
PZ7.R6185No   1999
[Fic]—dc21                                            98-26126

For my son-in-law Steven

# Contents

# Not *My* Dog

# Ellie

Ellie Martin had red hair and green eyes. She also had one hundred and twenty-four freckles. At least the last time she counted she did.

She had a mother who made quilts and a father who was a lawyer and played the bagpipes when he wasn't working. She had a fourteen-year-old sister named Karen, who was sometimes a pain.

Ellie lived in Baltimore. She had a grandmother and grandfather in Washington, D.C., and a grandmother and grandfather in Norfolk, Virginia. She had a bike of her own and a backyard with an apple tree in it.

She had a best friend named Amy, with whom she sometimes played after school and on weekends. Amy was going to be her partner when their class went on its trip to the zoo at the end of April.

But Ellie didn't have a puppy.

And she wanted a puppy more than anything she could think of.

Ellie told Amy, and even Billy Watson from around the corner, about the puppy she was going to have someday. She told the other children in her class and Mrs. Sweeney, her teacher, and the checker at the supermarket and the man who came to read the electric meter.

She went to the library and brought home books called *Raising Your Puppy, You and Your*

*Puppy,* and *How to Have a Healthy, Happy Pup.* After she read the books, she got out a piece of paper and made a list:

*Things I Will Do for My Puppy*
*(When I Get Him)*

1. *Name him something special*
2. *Give him food*
3. *Give him water*
4. *Teach him to come and sit and stay*
5. *Take him for a million walks*
6. *Play with him*
7. *Love him a lot*

Ellie drew pictures of the puppy she was going to get. The pictures didn't always look the same, though, because she wasn't sure what *kind* of dog would be the best.

Sometimes she wanted a puppy that would grow up to be a very large dog with a deep bark, like a Great Dane or a German shepherd. Other times she wanted a puppy that would grow up to be a very small dog with a yappy bark, like a miniature poodle or schnauzer.

But no matter what kind of dog her puppy grew up to be, Ellie knew he would tumble and skid across the floor, his toenails making clicking sounds against the wood. She knew he would play ball with her and curl up next to her to sleep. That he would tug at her sleeves and give puppy kisses and go for walks at the end of a new red leash.

"How soon can I *get* my puppy?" Ellie asked over and over.

"When you're nine," said her mother.

"When you're nine," said her father.

"When you're nine and old enough to take care of a dog of your own," said her mother.

"But I'm old enough *now*," Ellie always

said. Even when she was six and seven and eight.

One night in late April, while the family was having supper, Mr. Martin cleared his throat, the way he did when he had something important to say. Mrs. Martin cleared *her* throat, the way she did when she had something important to say.

"Now, Ellie," said Mr. Martin. "Today we had a letter from Great-aunt Margaret, and she said she's going to have to move from her big house into an apartment. She wants us to do her a favor."

"And," said her mother, "even though you're not quite nine, this will be your chance to have something you've always wanted."

"A puppy! I'm finally going to get a puppy!" cried Ellie. She could almost hear

little toenails clicking on the floor, could almost feel the puppy kisses. "But what did
Great-aunt Margaret have to do with getting
you to change your minds?"

"Well, we didn't exactly change our minds,"
said her mother.

"You see, it's like this," said her father.
"Great-aunt Margaret has asked if we will
take her dog because the building she's moving to doesn't allow dogs."

"You mean I'm getting a *dog* instead of a
*puppy*?" said Ellie, feeling a big, sad lump in
her throat. "But will I still get my puppy, too?
When I'm nine?"

"We were thinking that this would take
the place of the puppy," said her mother.
"But he can be yours, and you can do all the
things you have on the list of things you'll do
for a puppy—feed him, play with him, and
take him for walks. And we're sure you'll love
him just as much as you would a puppy. Be-

sides, your father and I think that one pet in the family is enough."

"A dog is better," said Karen in her bossiest, most know-it-all voice. "A dog doesn't wet the floor or chew slippers or dig holes in the flower bed."

"Or give puppy kisses, either," said Ellie, her voice small and squeaky.

"Great-aunt Margaret would feel just awful if she had to give her dog to strangers," said Karen.

"She really wants us to take him," said Dad.

"But we're strangers," said Ellie. "I don't even know Great-aunt Margaret, and she lives in another town and has never ever come to visit."

"We're family," said Mom.

It was so quiet in the room that Ellie could hear the clock tick. "Well, what do you think?" her mother asked. But the tone in her voice said that it didn't matter what Ellie thought. Her mother and father had already decided.

"Karen's right," said Dad. "It would make Great-aunt Margaret very sad to think that no one wanted her dog."

It makes *me* really sad that we have to take some boring old dog who probably can't do anything, Ellie thought.

"Well?" said her father.

"Okay, I guess," said Ellie in that same small, squeaky voice.

# Preston

The following Saturday, Mom and Dad and Ellie drove to Great-aunt Margaret's house in Hagerstown, a place that was an hour and a half away. Karen stayed behind to go to a rehearsal for her class play.

The whole time they were in the car, Ellie stared out the window and tried to pretend that she was going someplace else—to the beach or the pumpkin farm, or maybe to the zoo with Amy and the rest of her class.

"What's the dog's name?" she asked when they had been driving for a very long time.

"Preston. The dog's name is Preston," her father said.

"Preston?" said Ellie, thinking about the first thing on her list, the one that said, *Name him something special*. "Preston's not a special name. Besides, it's not even a regular *dog* name. Dogs are named Pongo or Pal or Prince. Dogs are named Rex or Rover or, sometimes, Sandy."

"Preston is a fine name for a dog," said her mother. "Anyway, it doesn't matter what his name is because I'm sure that Preston is a very nice dog."

"What *kind* of a very nice dog?" said Ellie.

"Hmmmmm, you know, I'm not sure," said Dad. "And when I called to tell Great-aunt Margaret that we'd take Preston, she didn't say."

"Maybe he's a Dalmatian," said Mom. "Or a golden retriever."

"No," said Ellie. "Dalmatians aren't named Preston. Or golden retrievers, either."

"Maybe he's a poodle," said Dad. "Or a German shepherd or even a cocker spaniel."

"No," said Ellie, thinking hard. "He's probably a sort of square, boring brown dog with sticking-up ears and a skinny tail."

"Whatever he looks like, I'm sure we'll like him," her mother said.

I'm not so sure, Ellie thought. She closed her eyes and wished she was home with Karen, going to the play rehearsal or even doing homework.

Mrs. Martin parked the car in front of a white house with green shutters. Ellie and her parents went up onto the porch and rang the bell. From the other side of the door came a deep rumbling bark that sounded a little bit like thunder and a little bit like the downlow keys on a piano.

Maybe he *is* a Dalmatian, thought Ellie, crossing her fingers and hoping. If she couldn't have a puppy, then maybe a full-grown Dalmatian with a rolling bark would be the next best thing. Or even a German shepherd or a Great Dane.

Great-aunt Margaret opened the door. "Hello, hello," she said in a chirpy voice. "I knew you'd be along any minute. I was just saying that to Preston, that you'd be here any minute. Bill and Helen—and Ellie," she said, kissing all three of them. She put her hand on Ellie's shoulder and said, "I remember one time when you were a very small girl. Your mother and father brought you to visit, and you and I had a fine time on that swing right over there, on the corner of the porch."

Then Great-aunt Margaret stepped back, saying, "Here's Preston," and making room for a sort of square brown dog with sticking-up ears and a skinny tail.

Boring, said Ellie to herself.

"Wonderful. He's wonderful," said her mother, reaching down and scratching Preston behind one ear. "It's really a shame that you have to give him up."

"Yes, yes it is," said Great-aunt Margaret, and her voice didn't sound chirpy anymore. "But this house is too much for me to manage, and, as I wrote you, I've found a nice apartment, but they don't take dogs."

Great-aunt Margaret led the way into the kitchen. She put a plate of cookies on the table and poured coffee for the grownups and apple juice for Ellie. She gave Preston a dog biscuit. "I would have given Preston to my great-grandson, but he's allergic to dogs and sneezes and sneezes whenever he's here for very long."

Allergic to dogs, thought Ellie, rubbing her nose. Maybe I could be just a little bit allergic to dogs, and then Great-aunt Margaret would have to give Preston to someone else. And by the time I'm nine, I could be cured of my allergy and get a puppy.

She rubbed her nose again and blinked her eyes. She pretended to sneeze.

Her mother looked at her the way she always did when she wanted Ellie to stop doing something. Then Mrs. Martin looked at Great-aunt Margaret and smiled. "Well, we don't have to worry about that. Nobody in our family is allergic to anything," she said.

The grownups visited for hours, and the whole time they were talking Ellie watched Preston. And the whole time *she* was watching Preston, *he* was watching Great-aunt

Margaret—as if he knew that something important was about to happen.

When it was time to go, Great-aunt Margaret gave Preston's big, round blue-denim
bed to Mr. Martin so he could put it in the
car. She put Preston's bowl, his red rubber
ball, his brush, a sack of kibble, and a box of
dog biscuits in a shopping bag. She handed
the bag to Ellie. Then she hooked one end of
Preston's leash to his collar and stood holding
the other end as if she didn't know what to
do next.

"You will let me know how he's doing,
won't you?" Great-aunt Margaret said. Her
voice sounded thin and shaky.

"Oh, of course," said Ellie's mother. "We'll
take very good care of him. Won't we, Ellie?"

Ellie nodded and watched as Great-aunt
Margaret handed the end of the leash to her
mother. Great-aunt Margaret kissed Ellie's
mother and father. She kissed Ellie. She bent

down to pat Preston, and as she did, Ellie was sure there were tears in the old lady's eyes.

Great-aunt Margaret turned away for a minute before she said goodbye.

# Ellie and Preston

On the way home, Ellie sat on one side of the backseat and Preston sat on the other. Ellie looked out her window, and Preston looked out his.

"I think Preston wants to go back where he came from," she said after a while. Her mother and father were busy talking to each other and didn't hear her, so she said it again. "I think Preston wants to go back. Let's turn around and take him there."

"Can't do that," said her father.

"But I think Preston is *sad*," said Ellie. "I think Great-aunt Margaret was sad, too."

"I'm sure she was," said Mr. Martin.

"It's very hard to give away a pet," said Mrs. Martin.

"Why did she, then? Give him away, I mean," said Ellie. "Why does she have to move?"

"We've been through all this before, Ellie," her father said. "Great-aunt Margaret is getting old, and it's too hard for her to take care of her house. It's hard for her to get someone to cut the grass in summer and shovel the snow in winter. But when she looked for an apartment, she couldn't find one that would let her take her dog."

"That's why we wanted to help her out," said Ellie's mother.

Ellie looked at Preston again. Even though she felt a little bit sorry for him, she wished someone else had offered to take him in. Be-

cause he wasn't a puppy, and he wasn't her
dog.

"Welcome home, Preston," said Mr. Martin as he carried the dog's bed into the house
and put it on the floor in the family room.
"This will be a good place for you to sleep."

Mrs. Martin poured some kibble into a
bowl and put it on the floor. Preston just
looked at it and turned away.

She rolled his red rubber ball across the
room. Preston watched it go and turned
away.

Mr. Martin patted the middle of Preston's
bed, calling, "Here, boy. Come over here."
But Preston sniffed it once and turned away.

After a while, Preston climbed up onto the
window seat and looked outside.

"That dog looks sad," said Karen when she
came home from rehearsal. "That dog looks
*really* sad."

Same as I do, only nobody cares, said Ellie to herself, putting on her scowly face and sliding down low on the couch.

When Ellie went to bed that night, she closed her eyes and tried to think about the perfect puppy, maybe one with curly hair and soft floppy ears and a stubby tail. But no matter how hard she tried, all she could think of was the way Great-aunt Margaret had looked when she said goodbye to Preston. And she wondered if right this very minute Great-aunt Margaret and the sort of square, boring brown dog with sticking-up ears and a skinny tail who was downstairs in the family room were thinking about each other.

As soon as Ellie got home from school on Monday, her mother asked her to take the dog for a walk. "Stay right on this block, though, so I can see you when I look out," Mrs. Martin said.

"Okay," said Ellie as she hooked Preston's leash to his collar and took him outside. They went to the corner and back, and Preston sniffed at trees and bushes along the way. Ellie scuffed her feet and wished that he would hurry up.

When Ellie and Preston came inside, Mrs. Martin said, "Oh, I wanted you to keep him out longer than that. Why don't you take him out again, and this time you could even run him up and down the block. The dog needs exercise. And so do you."

Ellie sighed and picked up the end of the leash. "Okay," she said. "Come on, Preston."

"And Ellie," her mother added, "why don't you call Amy when you get home and have her come see your dog?"

"That's okay, Mom. Not today. Anyway, I'm pretty sure Amy has something to do— like practice the piano or go to the store with her mother."

When she got to the sidewalk, Ellie didn't feel like running. So she walked Preston first to one corner and then to the other. Back and forth. Back and forth. All along the way, Preston sniffed at bushes and trees again, and Ellie thought about how she didn't want Amy to come over today or maybe any other day. How she'd talked so much about getting a puppy that she didn't want *anyone*—not Amy or Billy Watson or the other kids in her class or Mrs. Sweeney or the checker at the supermarket or even the meter reader—to see her with a plain ordinary *dog*.

"What's that?" shouted Billy Watson as he came around the corner on his bike. "What's that at the end of the leash?"

"A dog," said Ellie. "What's it look like?"

"Your dog? Is that *your* dog? What's his name?" said Billy, stopping his bike and getting off.

"His name is Preston. He's my Great-aunt Margaret's dog." Ellie crossed her fingers and went on. "He's just staying with us for a while."

"How long a while?" asked Billy.

"A little while," said Ellie.

"And where's your Great-aunt Margaret now?" said Billy.

"She's moving from her big house to an apartment," said Ellie.

"Where I bet she can't have a dog, so now he's yours forever," said Billy. "Right?"

"He's not. He's not," said Ellie, though she knew that Preston had come to stay forever.

"I thought you were going to get a puppy," said Billy, walking all around Preston and looking at him. "A little fluffy puppy is what you said. And you were going to train it and teach it to come and sit and stay. You always said that, too."

"I did. And I will," said Ellie in a big loud

voice, even though her mother and father had said they couldn't get a puppy now that they had a dog. She tugged on Preston's leash and started up the street to her house.

"Come on, Preston. Let's go," she said, looking back at the dog, who was sniffing a bramble bush.

"I bet she really misses him, your Great-aunt Margaret and Preston, I mean," yelled Billy. "And you know what? My grandmother has pictures of all the dogs she's ever had, in frames and lined up on a shelf in her family room. And when I go over there, she sometimes tells me stories about each one of them. Do you think your great-aunt has a picture of *him*?"

"Sometimes I can't stand Billy Watson," said Ellie under her breath. And I don't care what his grandmother has and I *will* get a puppy someday." She sat in the middle of the family-room floor, rolling Preston's red rubber ball back and forth from one hand to the other.

"It's not fair the way everybody in my family, including bossy old Karen, has decided that just because I wanted a puppy Preston should be *my* dog. But he's not *mine*," she said out loud, her words making a hissing, spitting sound.

With that, she rolled the ball as hard as she could into the far corner of the room.

Preston perked up his sticking-up ears even higher. He wagged his skinny tail. He ran after the ball and brought it back, dropping it in Ellie's lap.

"Ugh—dog slobber!" Ellie cried, looking at the ball. "Dog spit."

Preston just tilted his head to one side and put a paw on Ellie's arm. Come on, it's your turn now, he seemed to be saying.

Ellie picked up the ball and rolled it into

the corner of the room. Preston brought it back, his toenails making clicking noises on the floor.

Finally, Mrs. Martin came to the door and said, "Ellie, take your dog outside to play that game."

"Okay. But he's not *my* dog," said Ellie as she picked up the ball and headed for the door.

That night, after she had finished her homework and before it was time to go to bed, Ellie drew a picture of Preston. She used her brown marker for his fur and his sticking-up ears and his skinny tail, and a black marker for his eyes and nose. She gave him a big red mouth that looked as if it was smiling. Then she took hold of Preston's right front paw and held it down on the paper and traced around it with the same red marker.

Across the top of the paper she wrote *Here's Preston* in squiggly letters.

"This is for Great-aunt Margaret, so she won't forget what Preston looks like," said Ellie, holding up the picture for her parents to see.

"What a good picture, and what a good idea," said Ellie's mother.

"Now, why don't you sign your name, so Great-aunt Margaret will know who the picture is from," said her father as he pulled a large brown envelope out of the desk and handed it to her. "I'll mail it in the morning."

# No Zoo Today

On Thursday night, Ellie awoke with a stomachache. She threw up three times. Each time, her mother wiped her face with a cool washrag and gave her a cup of water to rinse her mouth with.

"Don't swallow it," Mrs. Martin said. "We want to give your tummy a rest."

And then, each time, she put Ellie back to bed, pulling the covers up under her chin.

The last time Ellie threw up, it was almost

morning. The sky was streaky with light, and the birds were beginning to chirp.

"I'm sorry, Ellie," said Mrs. Martin when she put her back to bed, "but you're not going to be able to go on your class trip to the zoo today."

"Not go to the zoo?" squeaked Ellie.

"I'm afraid not," said her mother. "I want you to stay home and get all well."

"But I *am* all well," said Ellie. "I feel fine." She didn't, of course. Her stomach still felt wobbly, and sometimes she was hot and cold at the same time. "Besides, I really *want* to go to the zoo."

"I know you do, Ellie. You'll go next time," said Mrs. Martin.

"But Amy and I were going to sit together on the bus. We were going to take peanut-butter-and-banana sandwiches for our lunch and grape juice to drink." At the thought of

peanut butter and bananas and grape juice, Ellie's stomach did a sort of flip-flop. She swallowed hard and slid down under the covers.

After a while, Ellie heard the alarm clock ring in her parents' room. She heard the shower running in the bathroom and her father singing his morning song. She heard her mother go downstairs and the bang and clatter of dishes as the rest of the family ate breakfast. She heard Preston bark for his kibble.

Later in the morning, after Ellie had had a little nap, her mother came into her room. "Good morning," said Mrs. Martin. "Are you feeling better?"

"Yes," said Ellie, sitting up in bed and pushing the hair out of her eyes. "Can I get up now? Can I get up and get dressed? If I hurry, maybe I can get to school before my class leaves for the zoo."

"No zoo today," her mother said. "Put on your slippers and come downstairs. You can lie on the couch in the family room and watch a little TV. I'll fix you a glass of ginger ale."

Ellie put on her slippers and followed her mother downstairs. She sat on the couch, and her mother put a blanket over her and gave her a glass of ginger ale. She turned on the TV to a children's show about a tall and skinny schoolteacher who could make magical things happen just by rubbing the top of her head.

"Now," said Mrs. Martin, "I'm going upstairs to do some work. You call me if you need anything."

After her mother left, Ellie settled back against the pillows. She took a sip of her ginger ale and felt the bubbles tickle her nose. She thought about the class trip to the zoo and about Amy sitting by herself on the bus. She thought about all the animals she was not going to see and about the lily pads she was not going to jump on and about the pavilion in the children's zoo she was not going to eat lunch in.

Ellie tried to concentrate on the tall and skinny schoolteacher on the TV, and watched as she rubbed her head and made all the toys in the kindergarten room dance in circles. "This is a *baby* show," said Ellie out loud. "A stupid *baby* show." With that, she padded across the room to get the remote control.

Back on the couch, Ellie started to change the channels. *Click click click* and *click click click*. *Click click click* and— Shows spun by before her eyes: the news, a cooking show, more news, a woman singing a hymn, a judge tapping his gavel, and the tall and skinny schoolteacher again. Then a huge, hairy monster flitted across the screen, followed quickly by a gardening show.

Ellie leaned forward and stopped changing channels. Then she carefully clicked another button until she found the monster again. "Cool," she said, leaning back and pulling the blanket up under her chin.

The monster was gigantic, with fiery eyes and arms shaped sort of like flippers. He was running down a crowded street, chasing a woman with yellow hair, flattening cars and toppling city buses as he went. Every once in a while, he let out a deep, snarling roar. The background music was loud and throbbing.

All of a sudden, the rest of the house seemed very quiet, and Ellie felt lonely and a little bit scared. She picked up her glass and took another swallow of ginger ale, but that didn't help. She put her fingers partway in her ears and half closed her eyes, but *that* didn't help. She thought about calling her mother, but knew that she would make Ellie turn off the TV—and Ellie wanted to see what happened to the woman with yellow hair.

"Preston," she said in a low, shaky voice. "Are you in here, Preston?"

From across the room, Ellie heard the clink of Preston's collar. Preston got down from the window seat and came over to the couch. He poked Ellie with his nose, and after a while he jumped up beside her. He stood there for a minute. Then he turned around and around, until he flopped down and curled into a ball right against Ellie's legs.

Ellie thought it felt warm and safe to have him there. The house didn't seem as quiet anymore, or the music as loud—or the monster nearly as large. She reached down and rubbed one of Preston's sticking-up ears.

"But you're *still* not my dog," Ellie said as she and Preston watched the end of the show before drifting off to sleep.

That night, after the rest of the family had supper and Ellie had a bowl of chicken-noodle soup and some more ginger ale, the phone rang. Mr. Martin answered it. "It's for you, Ellie," he called. "Great-aunt Margaret wants to talk to you."

"To me?" said Ellie, going to take the phone. Then she said, "Hello?"

"Well now, Ellie," Great-aunt Margaret said in a kind of booming voice. "I just had to call and thank you for that wonderful portrait of Preston. I have it right here, hooked onto my refrigerator with my flower magnets."

"Oh, that's good," said Ellie.

"Yes," said Great-aunt Margaret, "and I could tell from your picture that you've discovered what a very smart dog Preston is. Something about the eyes and the tilt of his head. He really *is* a smart dog, you know. Why, my goodness, he always knew to tell me it was suppertime before I even had a chance to look at the clock, and whenever I misplaced anything he was sure to find it. He found my glasses, my knitting, and, once, even my telephone when I left it under a stack of newspapers." She laughed a booming laugh and went on. "I often said that if I ever managed to lose *myself*, Preston would find me."

Ellie giggled at the thought of Great-aunt Margaret lost under a stack of papers. She swallowed hard to stop herself from laughing and said, "I'm glad—that you liked the picture, I mean."

"Indeed I did," said Great-aunt Margaret. "And I'm sending one back for you to show to Preston. So he won't forget me."

# The Long Way Home

On Monday, after school, Ellie brought Amy home with her. "I guess it's time for you to see the dog we got from Great-aunt Margaret," she had said when Amy called over the weekend to tell her about the class trip to the zoo.

"What's he look like? Your dog, I mean," said Amy as the two girls crossed the street with the crossing guard and headed for Ellie's house.

"Well, he's brown and sort of square with

sticking-up ears and a long skinny tail—and he's not exactly *my* dog," said Ellie. "He just lives here, is all."

When the girls went into the house, Preston sniffed Amy all around and tugged at her shoelaces. Amy let him lick her fingers, and after he was finished she scratched him under his chin. "I think he's cute," she said, standing back and looking at Preston. "I think he's really cute."

"Maybe a little, I guess," said Ellie.

"He looks like he should be on television, or in the movies," said Amy. "A little bit like Benji and Lassie kind of rolled into one."

"Do you really think so?" asked Ellie, squinting at Preston as though she had never seen him before. "Benji *and* Lassie?"

"And Pongo, too, but without the spots and painted brown, and with ears that stick up," said Amy.

"Yeah, that too," said Ellie, slipping her

fingers under Preston's collar and leading the way into the kitchen, where her mother had milk and cookies waiting.

"Here's a letter that came for you today," said Mrs. Martin as she handed a fat white envelope to Ellie.

"Who's it from?" asked Ellie. She unstuck the flap and pulled out a piece of paper, unfolding it and spreading it carefully on the table. "It's Great-aunt Margaret," she said, running her fingers over a crayon drawing of a woman in a blue flowered dress, her gray hair pulled into a topknot with a knitting needle stuck through it. In red block letters across the top were the words FOR PRESTON AND ELLIE—SO YOU WON'T FORGET ME.

"Look, Preston. It's Great-aunt Margaret," said Ellie, holding the picture out for him to see.

"Do you think he knows who it is?" asked Amy.

"I'm not sure," said Ellie, "but he *likes* it." And the three of them watched as the dog licked the paper and gently nibbled one of the corners.

"Now, Ellie," said Mrs. Martin when the girls had eaten their snack and Ellie had re-arranged the school papers and party invitations and dentist-appointment cards on the refrigerator door to make room for Great-aunt Margaret's picture. "I'd like the two of you to take Preston for a nice long walk."

"But, Mom," said Ellie, "I just brought Amy home to see the dog, and now she's seen him and we want to go over to her house because Billy is going there, too. We need to practice our three-legged race for the school field day next week."

"Please, Mrs. Martin. My mom said to tell you that if you walk us over to my house, she'll bring Ellie home when we're done," said Amy.

"That's fine," said Ellie's mother. "I'll take Preston along for the walk."

"Can he stay? Can Preston stay?" said Amy. "He can help us practice for the race. My mom likes dogs, so she won't mind a bit."

Amy's mother was glad to meet Preston. She found an old tennis ball and threw it for him while Ellie and Amy and Billy took turns practicing three-legged races up and down the yard. Sometimes Preston chased the ball, and sometimes he chased the children, barking and nipping at their tied-together legs. But most of the time he ran along beside Ellie, no matter where she went.

After they finished playing, Amy and Billy and Ellie sat on the back steps to rest. Preston sat in front of them, but closer to Ellie than

to anybody else. Without thinking, Ellie reached out to him, ruffling his fur one way and smoothing it flat the other—over and over, until Preston half closed his eyes and started to nod.

"That dog's pretty cool," said Billy. "Better than *ours*, who mostly just sleeps and snorts."

"And tons better than our *cats*, who don't do anything," said Amy.

When it was time to leave, Billy's mother picked him up to go to the dentist. Amy's mother was talking on the telephone, and Ellie didn't want to bother her. "I'm going to go," she said to Amy, hooking Preston's leash onto his collar.

"You can wait, she won't be long," said Amy. "Except that if she's talking to my grandmother, she *might* be long."

"That's all right," said Ellie, heading for the gate. "I'll see you tomorrow."

"Okay, Preston," she said when they were

standing on the sidewalk in front of Amy's house. "Mom said you needed exercise, so now we'll take the *long way* home."

Instead of turning right, they turned left. They went to the end of the block, and to the end of the block after that. They turned left again. When they came to a circle, they went around it one and a half times before taking a road that shot off to the side.

After a while, Preston stopped to sniff at a forsythia bush. Ellie looked around. She blinked her eyes and looked again. Nothing was the way it should have been.

There were houses lined along the street, but Ellie had never seen any of them before.

There were cars in the driveways, but she had never seen any of *them* before.

And, down at the corner, there was a woman working in her yard. But Ellie had never seen her before, either.

She looked up and down the street and

around the corner, but she didn't know which way to go. The woman who had been working in her yard wasn't there anymore, and Ellie didn't have the nerve to knock on her door and ask for directions.

Her hands were suddenly sweaty. Her knees shook, and she sat down on the curb. When she tried to speak, there was a lump in her throat.

"Oh, Preston," Ellie said. "I *thought* I knew the way, but now we're lost and I don't know what to do next."

Preston sat down next to Ellie. He twitched his sticking-up ears and wagged his skinny tail. *Thumpeta—thumpeta—thumpeta—thump—*

He looked one way and then the other. He stood up and stepped back as far as the leash would reach. He barked.

Preston barked again and gave a sudden jerk. The leash slipped out of Ellie's hand,

and she had to jump up and run to catch it. When she was holding on tight, Preston started to run, barking from time to time. Ellie was pretty sure he was telling her to come along, to hurry up.

Preston raced down the road to the circle, where he went around one and a half times. Still pulling Ellie behind him, he turned right, and right again. He flew past parked cars and trees and a boy playing ball, past Amy's house, and all the way to the corner.

Preston turned right one last time, pulling Ellie halfway down the block until he stopped in front of the Martins' house.

When Ellie went into the house, she was half laughing and half crying. She told her mother what had happened, the words tumbling out of her mouth all in a rush. Then she sighed and said, "Great-aunt Margaret said she was sure that if she ever got lost

Preston would find her, and that's what he did for me. I was lost, and Preston saved me. He brought me home."

That night, after everybody's favorite supper of spaghetti and meatballs, with a special treat for Preston, Ellie's grandfather called from Virginia.

"What's new?" said Granddaddy when it was Ellie's turn to talk.

"Well," said Ellie, settling into the chair by the telephone. "Today, when I was at my friend Amy's after school and it was time for me to come home, her mother was busy on the telephone. That's when I decided to come home by myself, only when I tried to find the long way, I got lost instead. But Preston saved me."

"Preston? Do I know Preston?" Granddaddy asked.

"He's the dog Great-aunt Margaret gave us

because she was moving and couldn't take him with her," said Ellie.

"Preston sounds very smart and brave to me," Granddaddy said. "And you're very lucky to have him for your dog."

"He is smart, I guess, and brave, too," said Ellie. "But I'm still not exactly sure he's *my* dog."

# Maybe We Made a Mistake

That night, when Ellie went to sleep, she had a scary dream about being lost. In her dream she was coming home from Amy's by herself, and all of a sudden she was in the middle of an enormous forest. There were trees everywhere—tall swaying ones with branches that stretched across the sky and shut out the sunlight.

She came to a clearing and went around and around in circles, trying to figure out what to do next. Finally, she started down a path that led her back into the forest. Then she looked over her shoulder and saw a huge, hairy monster coming after her. His eyes were like fire, and his flipper arms swatted at tree branches as he lumbered along.

Ellie tried to run, but her legs felt heavy, as though they were made of stone. She kicked as hard as she could. She kicked again, even harder. Then she woke up.

The covers were in a heap on the floor, and the neck of Ellie's pajamas was damp and sweaty. She got out of bed and went through the hall, heading down the stairs to tell her parents about her dream. But when she got almost to the bottom, she stopped. Even though she knew it wasn't polite to eavesdrop on other people's conversations, Ellie sat down to listen. Because her mother and father were talking about her. And Preston.

"You know, even when Ellie was on the phone with her grandfather, she didn't sound totally *sure* about Preston. Maybe we made a mistake," said Mrs. Martin.

Just as she said that, Preston came out of the kitchen and partway up the steps to sit beside Ellie.

"Maybe we did," said Mr. Martin, "but we were both so sure Ellie would love having a dog. That after a while she wouldn't even mind not having a puppy."

Ellie dug her fingers into Preston's fur.

"I wish we could get her the puppy she's always wanted, but I really think *two* is *too* many dogs," said Ellie's mother.

"A puppy," whispered Ellie to herself. "Maybe I could still get a puppy." But saying the words didn't make her feel as happy as they used to.

"We'll have to try and find another home for Preston, then," said Ellie's father.

And when Ellie heard that, she felt as if

she had a big empty hole right in the middle of her stomach.

"It will be upsetting for Great-aunt Margaret," said Mrs. Martin.

"And I hate for Preston to have to move again," said Mr. Martin.

Ellie's mother sighed. Her father sighed. Then he started to talk about the weather and how maybe it would rain by morning.

"Come on, Preston," whispered Ellie, standing up and taking the dog by the collar. "Let's go upstairs."

Back in her room, she picked up the covers from the floor and pulled them around her as she got into bed. Preston climbed in beside her, resting his head on her leg. Ellie thought about Preston and how they went for walks together and played ball, and how he liked to sniff the bramble bush. She thought about how they'd watched the monster movie together and how he'd brought her home when she was lost, and how she was going to get a book from the library, so she could teach him to come and sit and stay.

She thought of her father saying that they might have to find another home for Preston.

All of a sudden Ellie got out of bed. Calling to Preston to follow her, she went down the steps and into the family room, where her parents were watching television.

"I don't want you to get rid of Preston," she said, squeezing in between the two of them on the couch. "I had this really bad dream and I came down to tell you about it, only when I got to the bottom of the steps I heard you talking, so I listened. And I definitely don't want you to get rid of Preston."

"You don't?" said her mother.

"Even though he's not a puppy?" said her father.

Ellie shook her head. "It's okay having him

here. It's better than okay. It's maybe even better than having a puppy."

Preston tilted his head and looked from one to the other before he settled down onto the floor in front of them.

After that, Ellie told her mother and father about her dream. But when she told it, the monster didn't seem as scary as he had before—or the forest nearly as dark.

# Who Is Preston?

The next day at school, Mrs. Sweeney, Ellie's teacher, said, "Now, boys and girls, this afternoon we're each going to write a story." She talked for a while about their stories: they could be funny or sad or serious. She told them they should use good strong words that said exactly what they wanted to say. She even talked about spelling and punctuation.

When she was finished, she picked up a piece of yellow chalk and wrote on the blackboard in big block letters: SOMEONE IMPORTANT IN MY LIFE. "That's the title of your story," Mrs. Sweeney said, tapping her fingernails on the words. "Meanwhile, think of who you want to write about."

Ellie thought. She thought during lunch and recess and even a little bit during spelling and math. She thought about her mother and her father, who were the most important people in her life, and about her grandparents in Washington, D.C., and about her grandparents in Virginia, who came to visit and took her to do special things. She thought about her sister, Karen, who was sometimes a pain but who sometimes took her to the movies and once even braided her hair in about a million braids.

When it was time to start writing, Mrs. Sweeney handed out pieces of fresh white paper. She asked if anyone needed to sharpen a pencil. Then she said, "Begin."

Ellie chewed on the end of her pencil and thought a little bit more. She looked around the room and listened to the clock making a twitching noise. She began to write.

Ellie wrote and wrote, until Mrs. Sweeney called out, "Time to stop."

"And now, who would like to read his or her story out loud?" the teacher asked.

Ellie stretched her arm up in the air as high as it would go and waved her hand back and forth. But Mrs. Sweeney called on Peter, who read a story about his father. Next she chose Elizabeth, who read a story about her twin sister. Then came Amy, who had written about her cousin in Seattle, and Billy, who recited his story without looking at the paper—all about his Uncle Mort, who played the drums.

Ellie put her hand up again, and finally Mrs. Sweeney said, "Okay, Ellie. Would you come and read your story for us, please."

Ellie went to stand in front of the black-board. She cleared her throat and read:

*Preston used to live with Great-aunt Margaret, but she had to move. Now he lives with us, and he's going to stay forever. Sometimes we play ball, and sometimes he sits on the couch next to me and watches monster shows or sleeps in my bed. Once he even took me home from being lost. Preston is smart and brave and could probably be on TV or in the movies. But mostly he is my friend.*

"That's very good, Ellie," said Mrs. Sweeney. "But you forgot to tell us who Preston *is*."

"Preston?" said Ellie. "Preston is my dog."

All the way home, Ellie thought about how she would read her story out loud to Preston. Later, when she had made a copy, the two of them would walk to the corner mailbox and send it off to Great-aunt Margaret.